Kirsten
THE CRYSTAL BRINGER

To Kirsten
With Love & Blessings

Lanette Gutierrez

LANETTE GUTIERREZ

ISBN 978-1-64114-143-7 (paperback)
ISBN 978-1-64114-144-4 (digital)

Christian Faith Publishing, Inc.
832 Park Avenue
Meadville, PA 16335
www.christianfaithpublishing.com

Printed in the United States of America

Foreword

Many of the world's cultures have a creature that has been invoked to assist parents in keeping their children under control and following that culture's social rules. In my Scandinavian community, we children were taught to fear the wrath of trolls. My neighbor, who was from Narvik, Norway, had an impressive collection of hand-carved trolls that stared at us from shelves that lined his living room wall. All of them were crafted with hideous faces peeking through thick mossy hair. Their feet were huge—the better to chase us with. Their noses were long and warty—the better to sniff out our hiding places. And their eyes were piercing—so piercing that they could see the motives hidden in our hearts and see the truth even when we tried to lie. As a child, I learned a healthy respect for the role of the troll in my world.

Trolls played a significant role in virtue instruction. Each troll had a distinctive negative personality trait. As we learned the story of each troll, we also learned that these negative behaviors led to negative consequences for the people in that environment and for the troll. In this story, Grådig, translated "the greedy one," demonstrates this type of traditional virtue instruction. May my grandchildren, great-grandchildren, and yours, as well, benefit from his story.

Long ago and far away in the rugged mountains of the Northern Kingdom, there lived a troublesome troll known as Grådig, the Greedy One. His focus in life was to jealously guard the entrance to Crystal Valley. It was here that God had placed a unique source of healing for all the beings of this frozen, forbidding corner of His creation. The crystals that lay strewn across the valley held glimmers of His healing power that were so powerful the night sky above the valley glowed with waves of shimmering light. It was Grådig's goal to horde all of this healing power for himself—even if it meant the people of the kingdom would suffer and maybe even die.

As he stood on a lonely ledge surveying this valley, Grådig chanted,

"Mine! Mine! These crystals are all mine!
I'll keep all their power so I can live a long, long time."

Sometimes, a desperate mother or father would scramble up the boulder-strewn slope below the narrow entrance of the valley, hoping for a chance to creep in and quickly snatch up a crystal to heal a sick child. But Grådig always spotted the invader and yelled in a threatening voice,

"Mine! Mine! These crystals are all mine!
I'll keep all their power so I can live a long, long time."

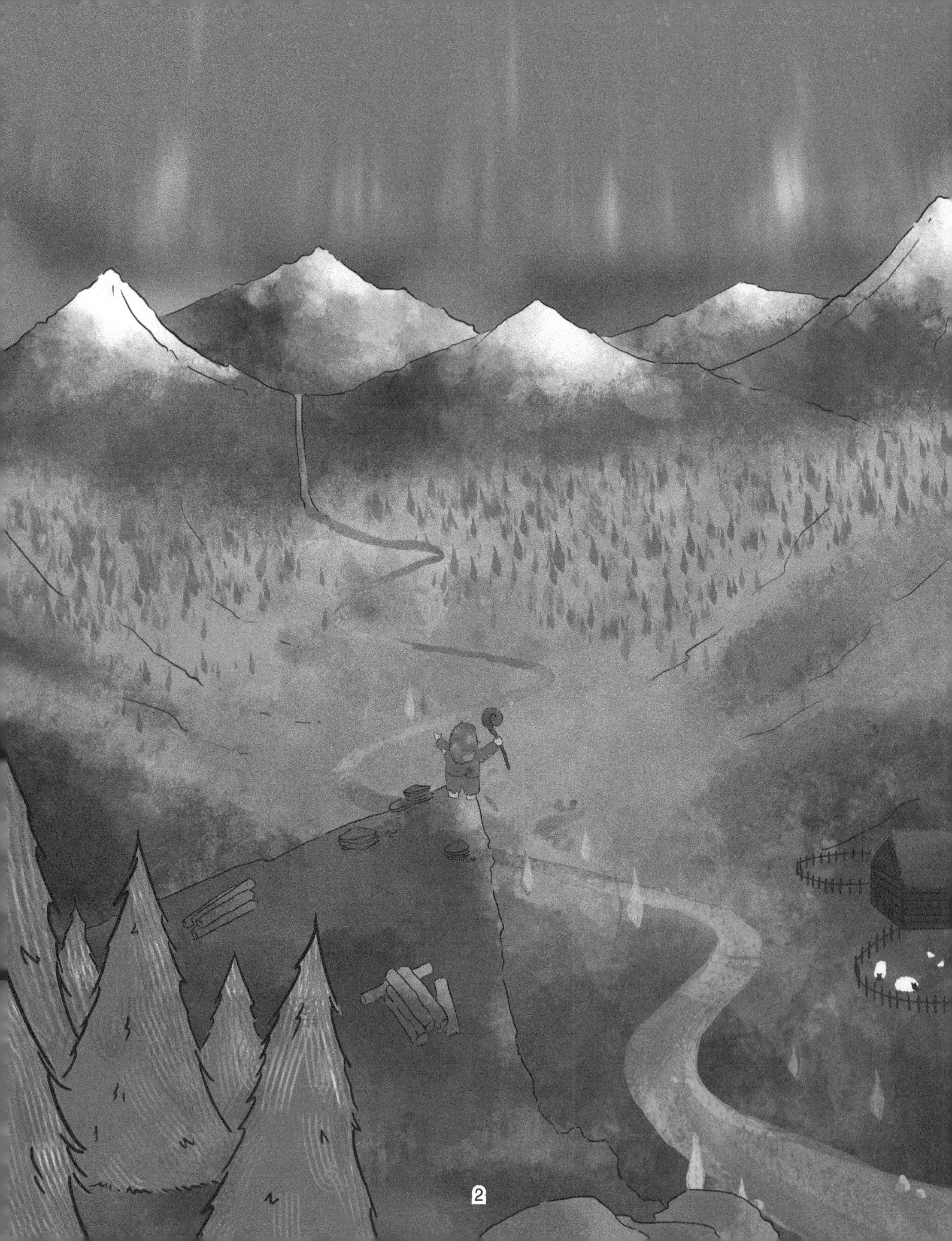

Then he would launch a fallen log or bulky boulder in their direction to force them to leave.

One day, an elderly woman crept from one tiny alpine tree to the next, hoping to escape the old troll's searching eyes. She was desperate for a crystal to heal her ailing husband. She almost made it to through the entrance when Grådig spotted her. "Please, please," she begged, "Just share one crystal here to save my husband's life."

Grådig just glared at her and shrieked,

"Mine! Mine! These crystals are all mine!
I'll keep all their power so I can live a long, long time."

She returned heartbroken to her dying husband.

A young farm girl known as Kirsten was working alongside her mother in the goat pen when her mother collapsed. Her father was away at sea with the fishing fleet. She alone must decide how to help her mother. First, she rolled her onto a strong blanket and pulled her into their warm hut. She tried gently shaking her mother's shoulder to wake her up. No response. She laid a warm cloth across her mother's head. No response. She cradled her mother's head and sobbed softly over her. No response.

"Whatever shall I do?" she asked herself frantically. Suddenly, she thought of the healing crystals in the valley above her farm. She drew on all her courage and decided that she must enter Crystal Valley. First, she dressed in grays and browns to act as camouflage as she ascended the slope. She stole as quietly as possible up the mountain slope slipping behind scattered boulders and between the alpine trees. Near the entrance of the valley, she looked up at Grådig's ledge and thought, Am I going to be in luck? It sure looks as if the old troll is snoozing to me. Not so.

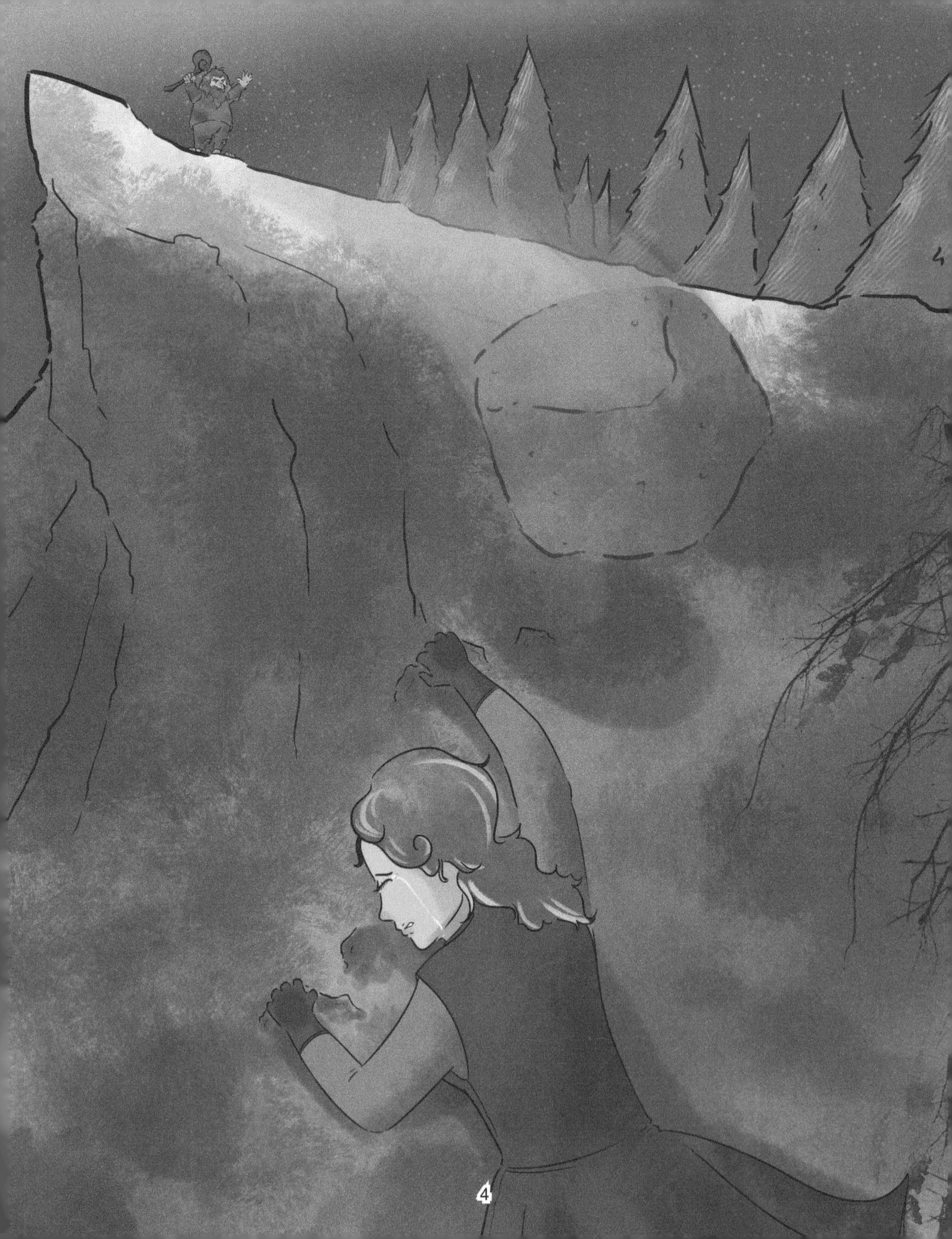

Her next movement near the entrance of the valley caught his attention. He roared,

"Mine! Mine! These crystals are all mine!
I'll keep all their power so I can live a long, long time."

With that warning, he heaved a heavy boulder so close to her she was nearly crushed. She returned home bruised and bleeding to find her mother dead. She collapsed weeping half with sadness for her loss and half with anger at the boulder-tossing, log-launching, tough old troll who had brought so much misery to the kingdom with his miserly ways.

Strangely enough even with good health and the promise of a long life, Grådig was not exactly happy. Those living in the farms below his mountain ledge or in the small village along the local fjord often heard his lonely lament . . .

Mosses, beetles, bugs, and slugs,
Mosses, beetles, bugs, and slugs,
These I eat a lot, but someday I hope to eat some rømmegrøt.

The aroma of this rich, creamy pudding must have wafted up to his mountain perch during local wedding celebrations or kingdom holidays. Of course, Grådig was so obsessed with guarding Crystal Valley that he never ventured down the mountain to barter one of his crystals for a bowl of this delicious treat. Any of the villagers would have been delighted to trade a big bowl of their pudding for the healing power of one of God's crystals. But this old troll was not about to change his ways . . . at least not just yet.

Chapter 2

The days following her mother's funeral were long and lonely for Kirsten. She spent her mornings in the company of three spotted goats, two wooly white sheep, and five golden hens. No dog, no cats. School did not exist here, nor did she even have a book to read—that is if she could read.

Her small hut hugged the mountain slope behind it. The heavy, timbered walls were topped with a shaggy sod roof. Because there was just one window facing toward the fjord below, the inside was often dark and full of shadows. The crackle of the wood stove added some light and a cozy warmth to this humble home.

As a farm girl, she had daily chores that must get done. The goats must be milked and then sent to graze on the grassy mountain slopes with the sheep. She cleaned their pens and brought in fresh straw, hay, and water for the evening. The hens were fed and watered after she gathered their eggs. Then they were set free to roam the dell surrounding the hut.

After breakfast, she took the goat's milk to make her breakfast cheese she called gjetost. She made her own bread from dark rye flour sold in the village. She often traded her extra eggs and cheese for what she needed there. When she had finished her daily chores, she would polish up her one window and gaze on the fjord below, hoping to catch sight of her father's fishing boat returning from the far North Sea. Again, today it did not appear, so she sent prayers of protection for her father to God above.

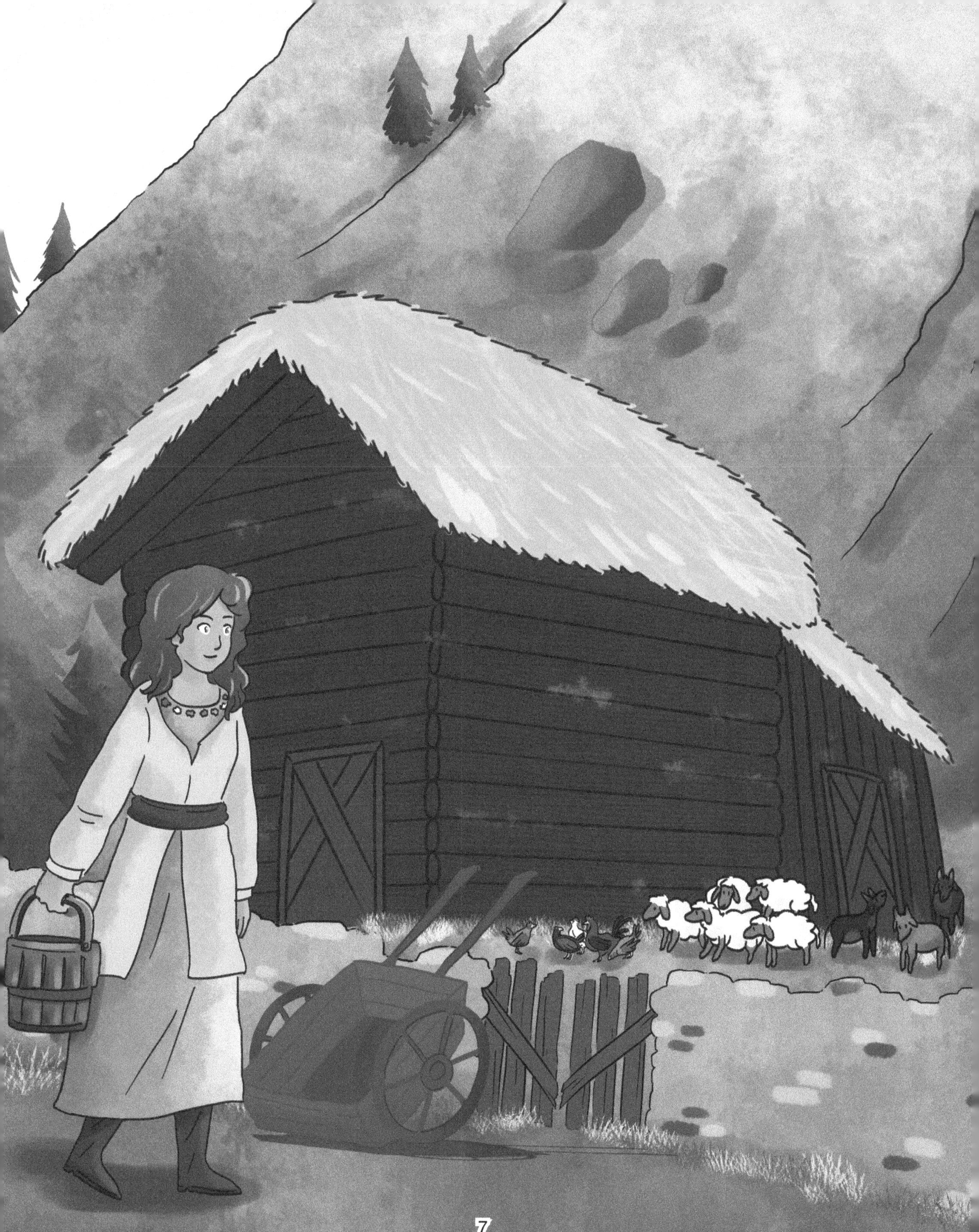

To pass the long afternoons, she often hiked into the forest just above her dell. Here a silvery waterfall plunged from the cliffs, spilling into an isolated pool at the woodland's edge. The sound of the falling waters seemed to wash away some of her grief and loneliness. Here at the pool's edge, she pondered the problems of her present life and even dared to dream of adventures beyond this valley and its tiny village. She never saw another human come to this place, but she sometimes heard the great Grådig rumble out his warning to all the area's inhabitants,

"Mine! Mine! These crystals are all mine!
I'll keep all their power so I can live a long, long time."

She did, however, share this pool with an immense grey heron. This impressive bird was so accustomed to her presence that he accepted her company without hesitation or fear. She often offered him treats of bread to add interest to his diet of frogs and small fishes from the pool. When he would see her approaching the pool, he would wade slowly toward her to accept the treat.

Soon she felt so comfortable with this bird that she began talking to him as if he were a trusted confidant. "I thank you for being my faithful friend, great heron. It is so easy to tell you everything that is on my mind and in my heart. You always listen with interest and concern! I am fortunate to have you share my life." His calm presence made her feel as if he understood her worries and her woes.

Occasionally though, the peace of that place was shattered by the lonely lament of the gruff old troll on the mountain ledge far above them . . .

"Mosses, beetles, bugs, and slugs;
Mosses, beetles, bugs, and slugs,
These I eat a lot, but someday I wish to eat some rømmegrøt!"

"You stingy old troll, you!" shouted Kirsten. "I'd have gladly made you a big bowl of rømmegrøt for one of God's healing crystals you so jealously horde. I

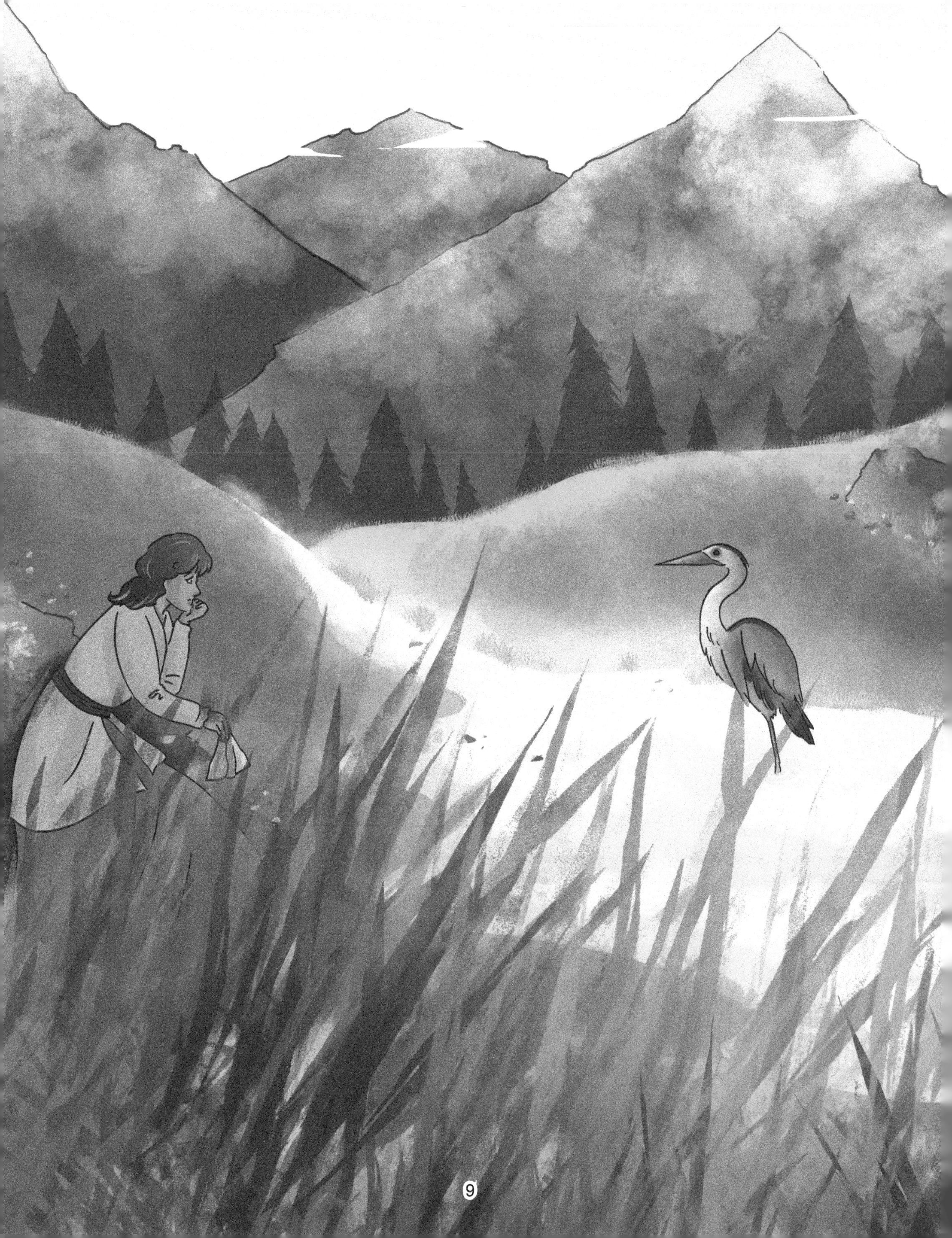

just needed one crystal with enough power to save my mother, but would you have any mercy on us? *No!* You are far too miserly for that, so stay miserable and eat bugs and slugs for all eternity for all I care!"

The heron, not put off by her ranting, moved closer to her as if protecting and encouraging her during her honest outburst.

"Someday, great heron, I see us flying away from here—together!"

Chapter 3

On a dark, damp day in November, the village watchman strode through the village and continued down the country lanes to the farms in the local dells. As he hurried along, his lantern swinging, he shouted a call to one and all, "Hear ye! Hear ye! Our beloved king is gravely ill. No doctor in the kingdom has been able to cure him. He implores the people of this place to enter Crystal Valley and bring a healing crystal to the castle just as soon as possible."

Their king was a wise, just, and compassionate man who was respected by all the citizens of the Northern Kingdom. His heir, the valiant Prince Gustaf, had voyaged far away to expand the kingdom by conquering villages to the south. He knew nothing of his father's illness, and no one knew exactly where he was or when he might return.

They worried and wondered who would dare to face the greedy Grådig. Who would come up with a successful plan for bringing a crystal down from the mountain? Many had tried, and all had failed.

Kirsten thought, *I know what Prince Gustaf would do if he were here. He would surely challenge and battle Grådig, even to the death to obtain a powerful healing crystal from Crystal Valley. I hope he never has to suffer the regrets I feel because of a beloved parent's death that could have been prevented by just one crystal.*

Later that day, Kirsten dressed warmly and hiked through the misty rain to the edge of the pool where she could think and maybe even come up with a plan. She sank down into the forest ferns still weeping with grief over the loss of her

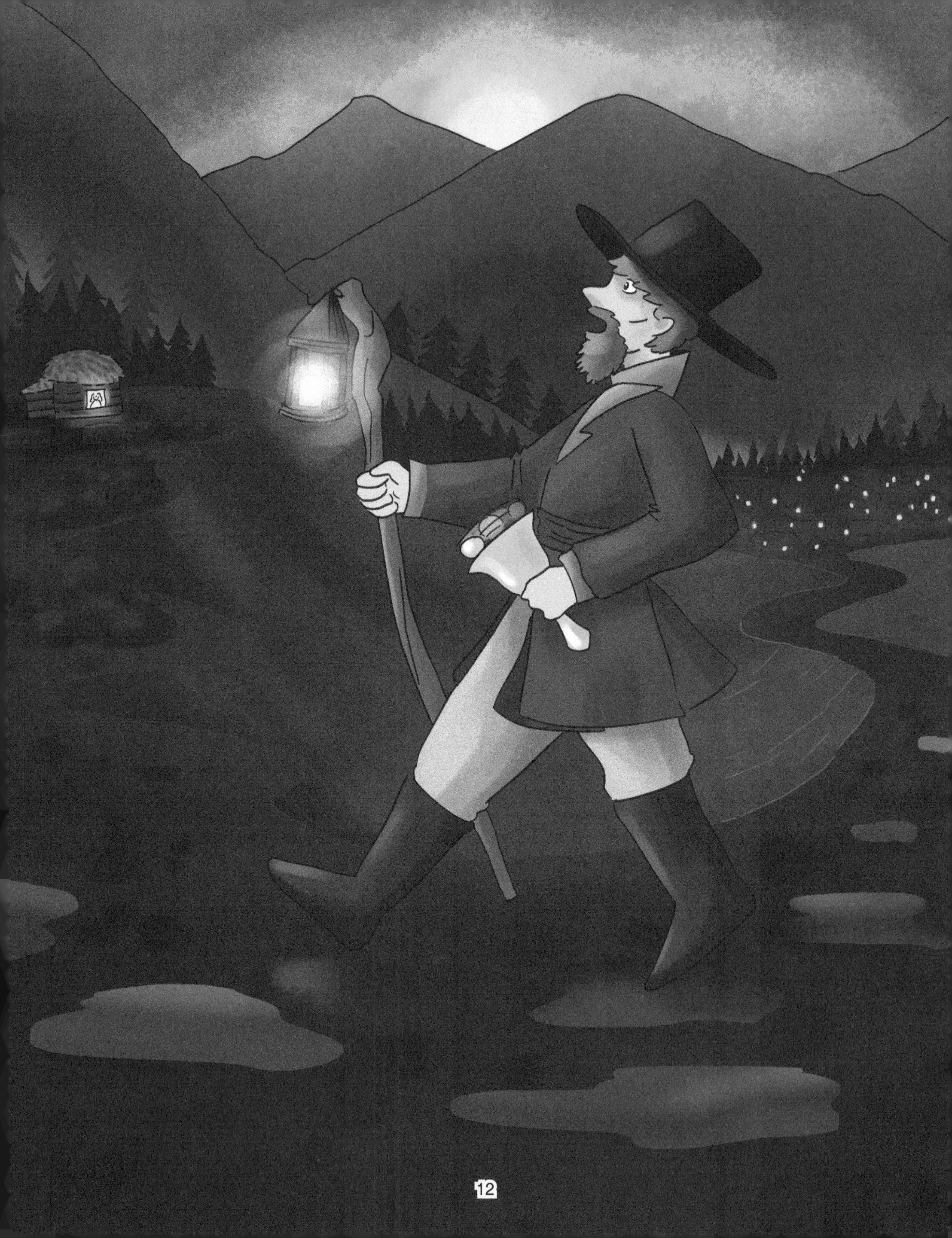

mother and worrying over the possible loss of her king. The great heron stood somberly nearby. Just then she heard the old troll chanting,

Mosses, beetles, bugs, and slugs,
Mosses, beetles, bugs, and slugs,
These I eat a lot, but some day I'd love to eat some rømmegrøt.

"That's it!" she exclaimed, startling the great bird. "For months, I have had a vision of flying away from here on your broad back. Today is so misty and gray that if I were on your back, we could fly into Crystal Valley, I could scoop up a crystal, and we would be on our way before Grådig could stop us. I think it could work! We must try!"

The great grey heron had been her sole companion for so long that he seemed to understand her plan; he certainly sensed her excitement.

He quickly stepped up beside her. She threw her arms around his long narrow neck and positioned herself safely in front of his mighty wings. After a few long strides, he was in the air gliding swiftly through the mountain mists to the valley above.

Grådig stirred at the edge of his ledge. He heard the strange beating noise of the heron's wings but could not see anything in the thick gray mists. Feeling that something was approaching the valley he claimed as his own, he yelled his warning,

"Mine! Mine! These crystals are all mine!
I'll keep all their power so I can live a long, long time."

It was then he spotted the huge grey heron with Kirsten nestled on its back swooping toward the valley's entrance. "No, no. I won't let you go!" screamed the troll. He hoisted a huge boulder over his head, hurling it directly at them. *Whoosh!* It flew right passed them, nearly knocking them from the air.

Immediately, Grådig flung a second boulder that came careening straight toward them. The heron veered to the right as the large stone narrowly missed crushing them. "This is too dangerous!" yelled Kirsten to her companion. "Let's go back to the village. I think I have a better plan." But what could that be?

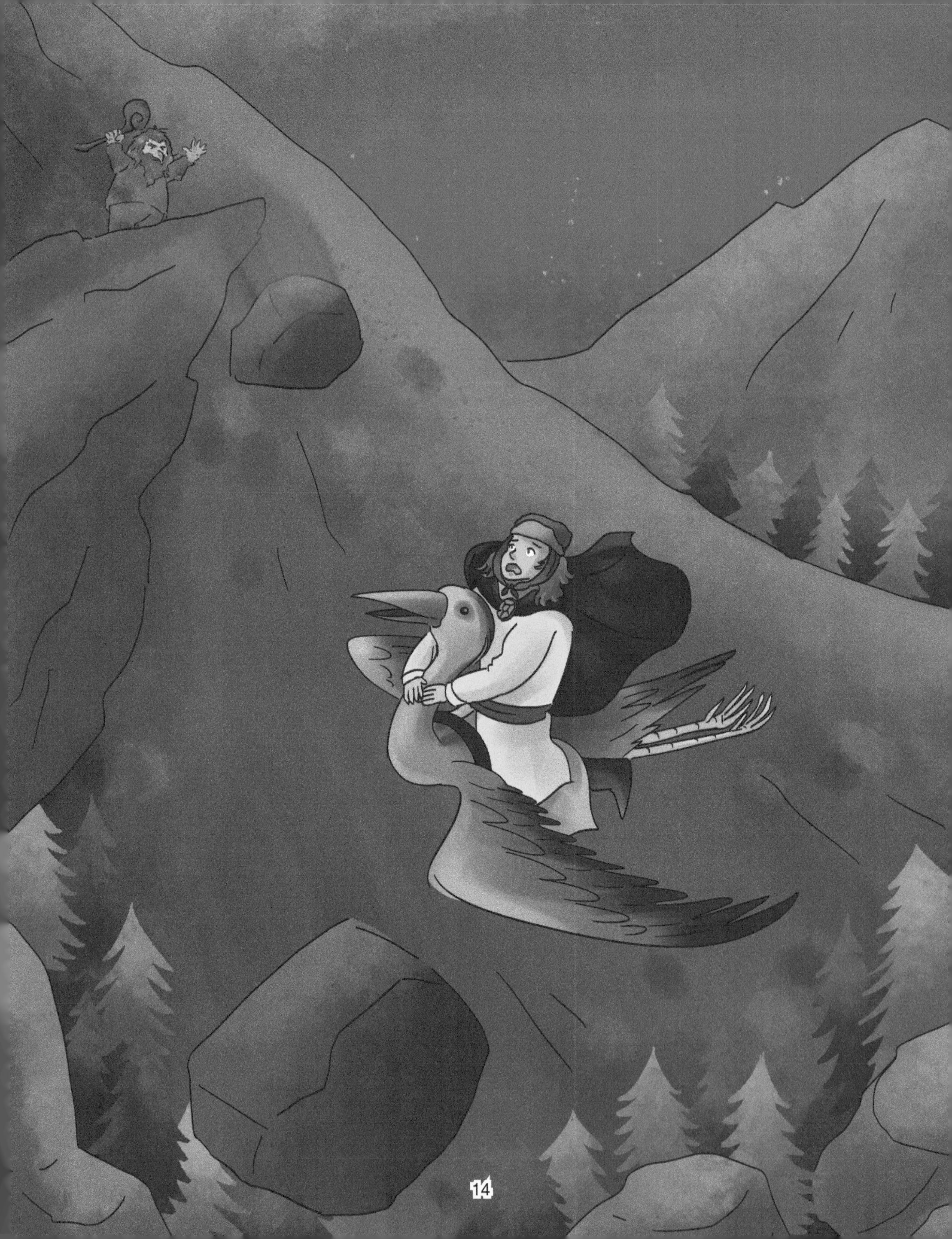

Chapter 4

The villagers stood gawking at the sky above them in awe and disbelief as the majestic grey heron circled the square.

"Why, could that Kirsten on the heron's back?" asked a young farmer.

Soon the heron skidded to a landing on the damp cobbles of the village square. Kirsten slid off the heron's back glowing with excitement. "I have a plan to save the king!" she announced boldly. "But I will need lots help from all of you."

"What plan could you have that could possibly succeed against Gràdig?" inquired a respected elder of the village.

"It's simply this! Most of you have heard Gràdig complain for years about how tired he is of eating mosses, beetles, bugs, and slugs. He always wishes for some of our creamy rømmegrøt. If we work together to surprise him with a bowl of this treat, I am sure that he will become so distracted by this unexpected treat that I am hoping he won't even notice as the heron and I fly far above him into Crystal Valley. Once I have scooped up a healing crystal from the valley floor, we will fly directly to the king's castle to present this lifesaving gift to him."

"Can you imagine how many lives could have been saved in our kingdom if we had thought of this plan before?" mused another village elder.

"Let's get started right away," urged a village housewife. "I think Kirsten has come up with an idea that just might work. We must try!"

A farmer left the square and soon returned with a large pail of milk and a jug of sour cream. The woodcutter loaded his cart with firewood; soon he had a

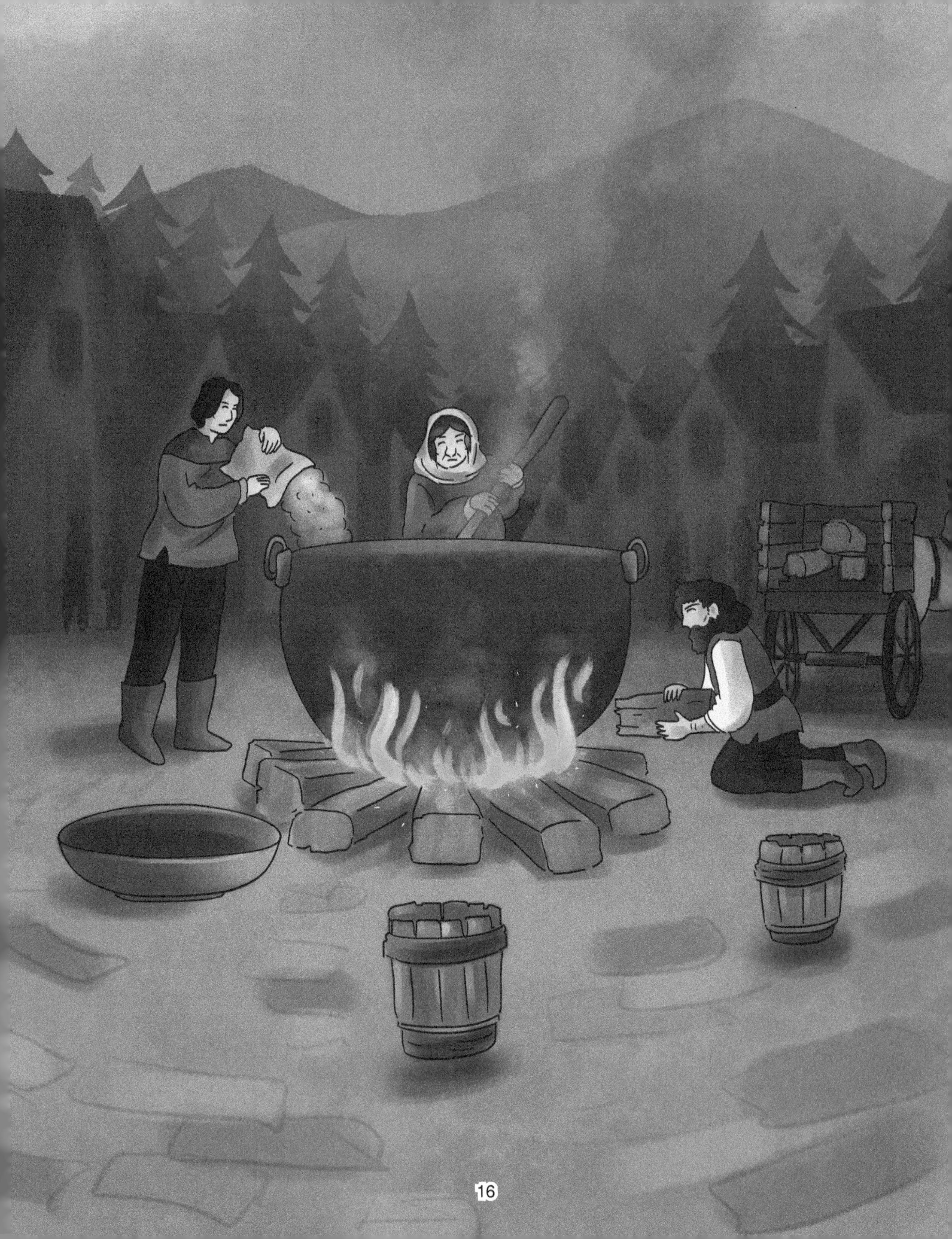

cooking fire going. The village miller ground a bag of his finest flour to thicken the rømmegrøt. A village housewife collected salt, cinnamon, and sugar from her kitchen cupboards. Meanwhile, the soapmaker scoured his finest black kettle and brought it to the cooking fire. A massive wooden bread bowl was found to serve this treat to the miserable old troll.

Soon the cream was cooking, causing the rich butterfat to rise in the kettle. After adding more wood to the fire, the milk came to a boil. The flour was blended into the milk, making it creamy and smooth. The cool fall air quickly caused the pudding to thicken. Finally, some villagers took some wooden paddles and piled the rømmegrøt into the wooden bowl.Lastly, a village wife topped the rømmegrøt with butter, sugar, and cinnamon.

"Now this dish is so tempting Grådig simply won't be able to resist it," declared an elder of the village.

"We need to get this bowl on its way before it cools too much," urged the woodcutter. He positioned his cart near the fire; three men steadied the bowl as it was positioned securely on the cart. Soon the woodcutter was urging his sturdy fjord horse up the road leading toward Grådig's ledge.

Grådig heard the noisy cart rumbling closer and closer to his mountain perch. He watched suspiciously as the people and the horse-drawn cart drew nearer and nearer to his lair. Suddenly, his nose caught the warm, creamy scent of rømme-grøt drifting up toward his cold, damp cave.

"What? Could this rømmegrøt be for me?" asked Grådig. "It's not the mid-summer festival, and there is no bride and groom."

The woodcutter explained, "For many years we have heard your lament, 'Mosses, beetles, bugs, and slugs. These I eat a lot.' So today we have made you this gift of rømmegrøt. Please enjoy it with our blessings."

Grådig could not believe his eyes or ears. After all these years of dreaming of this delicious dish, here was a great bowl of rømmegrøt prepared just for him. Tears welled up in his crusty green eyes as he edged his way to the cart and finally

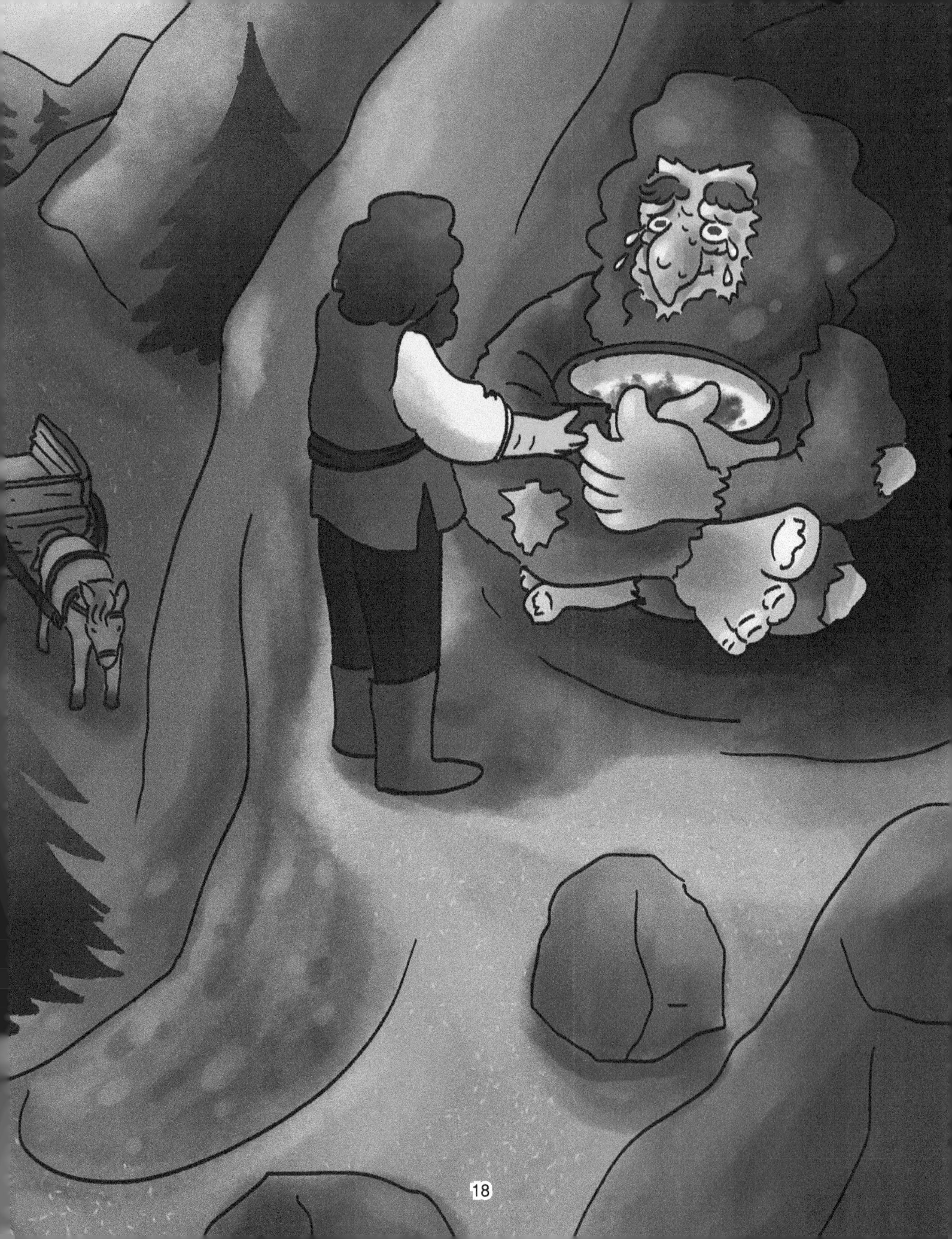

lifted the wooden bowl, cradling it in his arms, he brought it out of the misty rain and into his cave to enjoy.

"This is more delicious than I ever imagined," mused the old troll to the villagers below. "I thank you for your kindness."

As he gulped down large handfuls of his treat, would he even notice the heron and Kirsten soaring high above him through the narrow entrance to Crystal Valley?

Chapter 5

Kirsten hugged the heron's neck tightly as it swooped just above the trees, then glided quickly through the narrow entrance to the valley. "We made it," Kirsten exclaimed. "Grådig is so busy greedily guzzling his rømme-grøt that he didn't even notice us!"

Soon the heron gently descended toward the valley's meadow, which was strewn with softly glowing stones scattered through the wet grasses. The heron landed near the bank of a small brook where a fine group of the stones glimmered even in that day's dank fog. Kirsten quickly scooped up a stone that she felt was fit for her king. She dropped it in the leather pouch hanging from her neck as she quickly mounted the heron's back. In no time at all, they were on their way winging across wide expanses of misty gray forests, soaring over craggy mountain ridges finally descending to the coastal cliffs where the king's castle stood just above the sea's powerful waves.

Kirsten was shaking from the cold and damp flight, but on they flew over the fortress walls until they landed in the innermost courtyard where the king's guards were aghast at the sight of this gigantic bird swooping down upon them. They grabbed their bows and set their arrows against this strange pair invading their domain.

"*Stop!*" shrieked Kirsten as she slid from the heron's back.

"Who goes there, and why have you come?" challenged the captain of the guards.

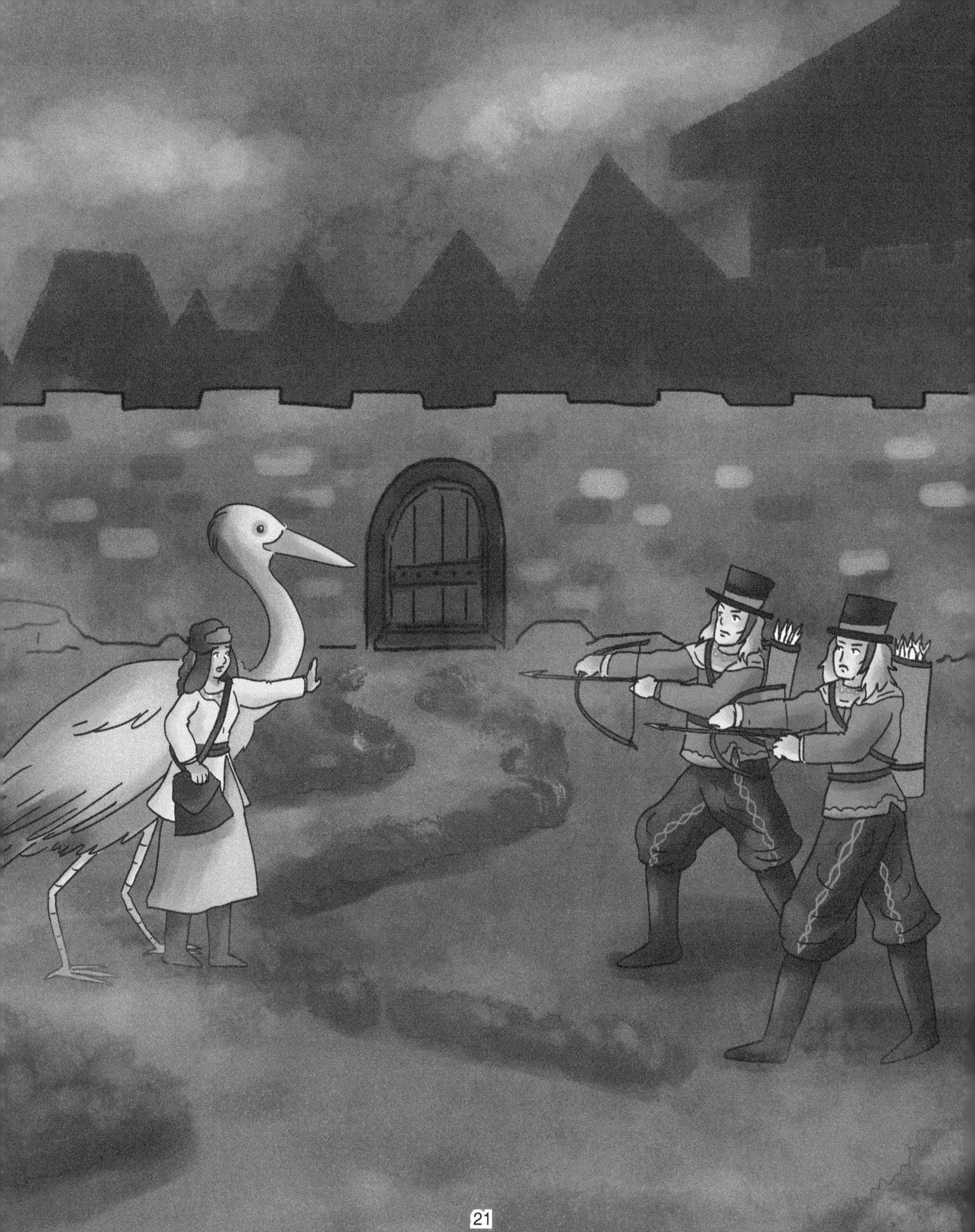

"My name is Kirsten, and I am a simple farm girl from the north," she proclaimed. "Here! I have brought the king a gift of healing power, a crystal from the valley long guarded by that greedy ancient troll, Grådig."

"But, then how did you come to ride this great grey heron?" queried one of the guards. "But, here, let's get you inside and warm you up first."

Later, Kirsten explained, "When my mother died, I spent many hours in the company of this grey heron at a pool we shared below the Crystal Valley. He has been my companion and my listening ear through many months of grief for my mother. It seems that after the months we have shared, he understands the intent of my heart and the meaning of my words. Without him, there would not be God's miracle crystal here now."

The guards escorted Kirsten into the king's quarters where she carefully presented the crystal to the king's physician; he immediately took it to the king's bedside.

Kirsten was given a room in the castle to warm herself and rest while the heron made himself at home near a courtyard pool which the guards had thoughtfully supplied with small fish.

Over the next month, the king gradually regained his strength, and by the following month, he was pronounced healthy and fit again. One of the first actions he took was to order his finest carriage to be readied to bring Kirsten back to her farm near the village below Grådig's mountain perch. The royal carriage with the great grey heron flying overhead made an impressive entrance into the small village.

For the villagers and nearby farmers, it was the first time that they had met their king. The king listened to their story of the intimidating Grådig and of Kirsten's fearless plan to trick the troll to get a healing crystal. The king held a great feast in honor of all that they had done on his behalf. He promised to return soon with a very special reward for Kirsten.

What could the king be planning for this simple farm girl? they all wondered.

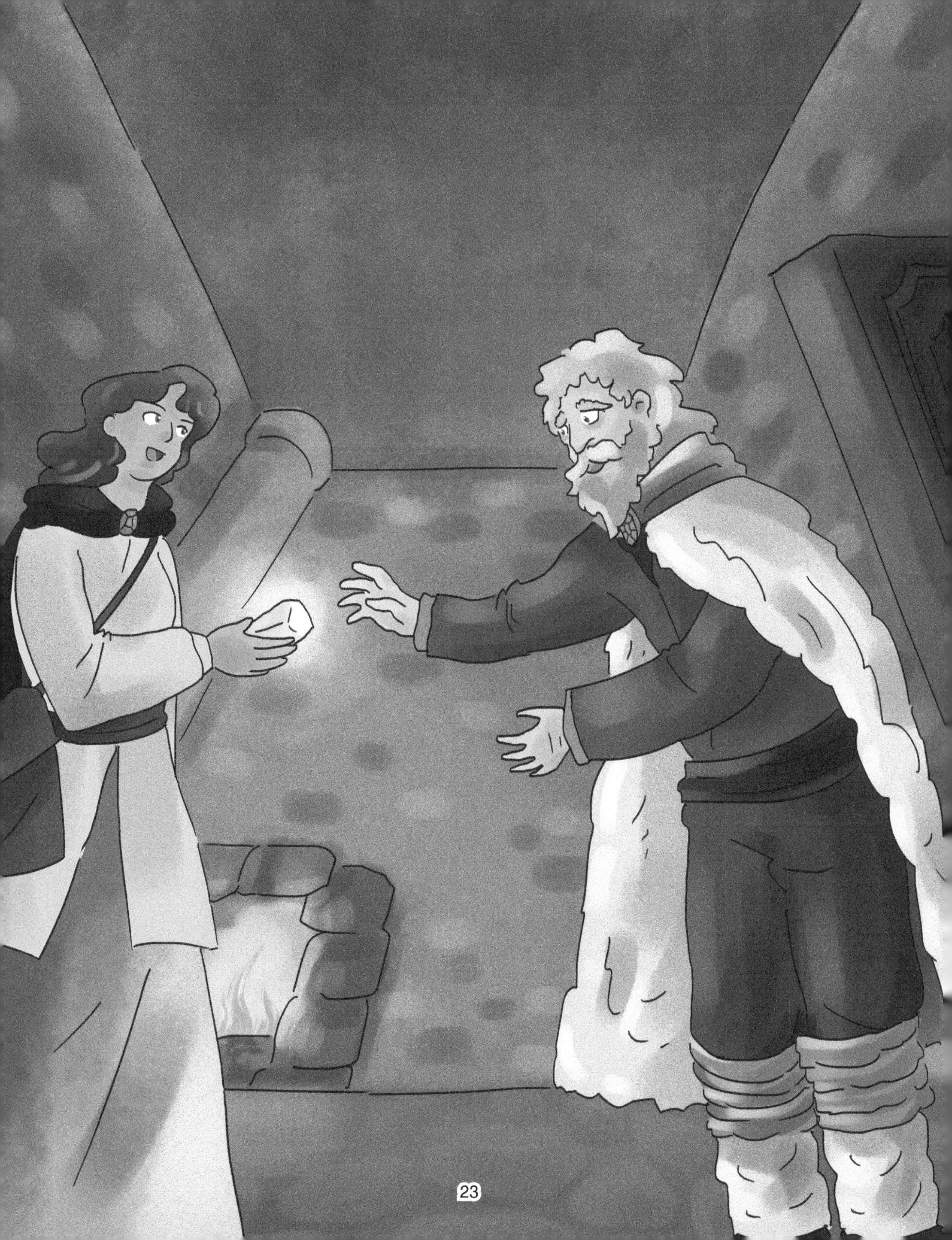

Chapter 6

Kirsten had returned to her quiet life on the farm and lonely hikes to the pool to visit her friend, the heron. She pondered the king's last words to her about a special reward to come to her. What could it be?

Meanwhile, Grådig thundered twice from the ledge far above them,

> Mosses, beetles, bugs, and slugs, these I eat these a lot,
> but someday soon I want some more rømmegrøt.

Each time Kirsten heard that chant, she would smile to herself and think, *Maybe that will happen more if you finally learn to share!*

As spring came and travel became easier in the mountains of the Northern Kingdom, the king prepared a coach to make a return journey to Kirsten's village. A wagon loaded with cooking pots, large bowls, and food supplies followed behind. As the procession entered the village, the local people, full of curiosity, gathered in the square. The king summoned Kirsten to hear of his plan for her.

"My brave young woman, it is because of you that I am here today. You saved my life with your bold plan. For this reason, I have come to ask you to be my chief advisor and assistant to the citizens of the kingdom who need healing.

"I have a wagon loaded with all but the cream and milk needed to make Grådig more rømmegrøt. Here I have this bag of gold to buy cream and milk from the

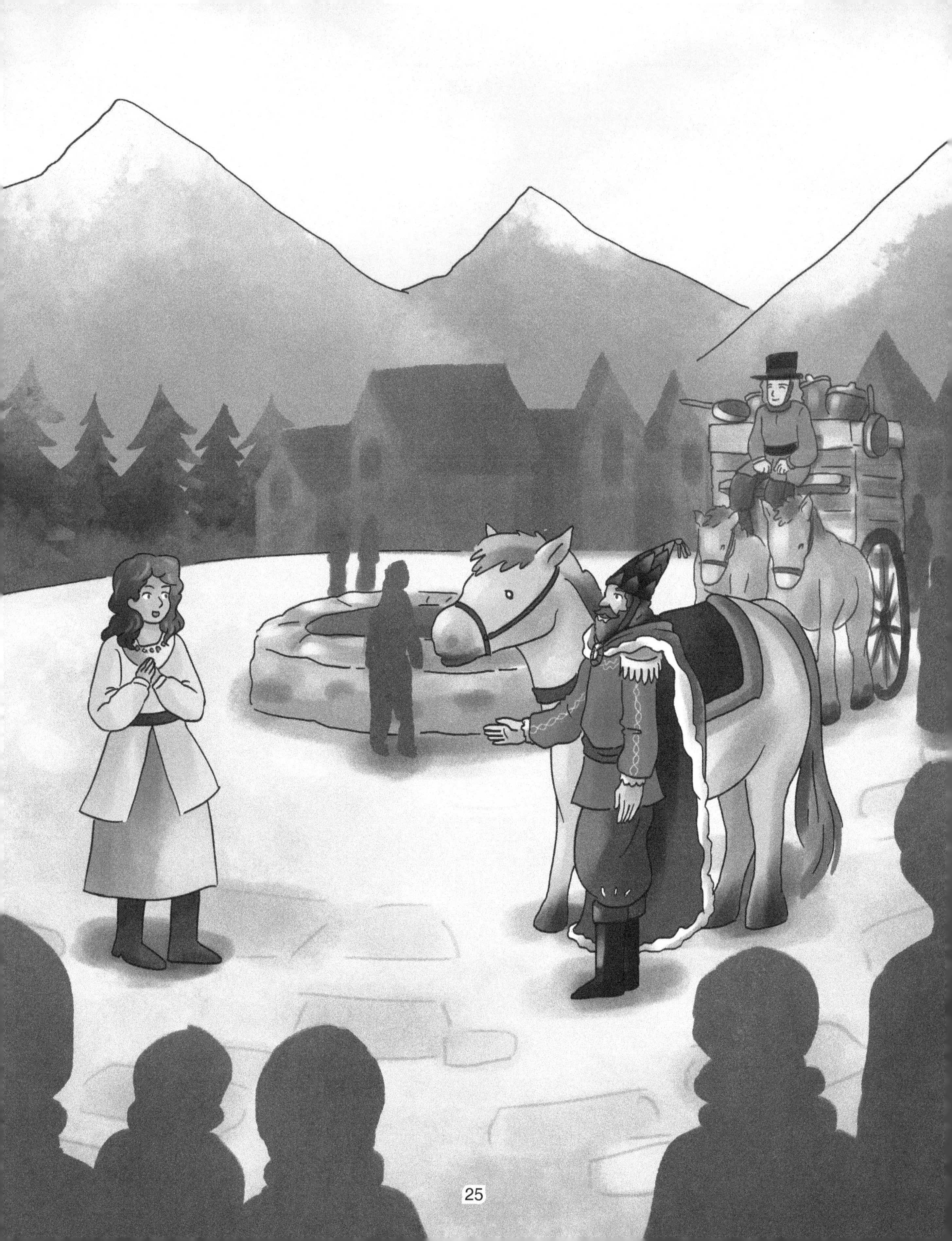

local farms. I am sure that you can save many lives in the years to come with more flights of mercy into Crystal Valley."

Kirsten now had the gift of a future filled with purpose and promise, but could she convince Grådig to cooperate?

She called the heron to her side and pointed to the ledge above. The heron gave her a look that asked, "Do you really want to do this? Remember the last time we flew by him when he was watching? We could have been smooshed by one of those boulders he lobbed at us!"

Her intuition told her it was time to test this troublesome troll and see just how badly he wanted some rømmegrøt. They swooped up the mountain slope and close to his lookout ledge.

"*Not again*, you tricksters, you! No more stealing my crystals! Not even for rømmegrøt!" shrieked the troll as he made a grab for the biggest boulder in his reach. He could barely hoist it above his shoulders, and when he threw himself forward to launch it into the air, he stumbled and fell over the edge of his ledge. He careened down the steep slope, crashing into boulder after boulder finally landing in a groaning heap.

"Oh, my!" shouted Kirsten, "he's groaning, so he did not die! Whatever shall I do now?"

Kirsten and the heron soon landed in the village square where a few of the villagers were already gathering after hearing the crash of the boulder and observing the old troll noisily careening down the slope."

"Now's our chance," yelled one villager. "Let him die where he lies!"

"For sure!" shouted a second villager. "He never showed any mercy for us. Why should we show mercy for him?"

All the villagers joined in condemnation of the suffering troll, except for Kirsten. She was thinking. Finally, she spoke to all who were gathered there. "If we have no mercy, we are treating him no better than he has treated us. Are we trolls that we should behave as he has? As the king's advisor, I have a different idea."

She summoned the heron and flew off to Grådig as the villagers shook their heads. Upon landing near the fallen troll, Kirsten spoke sharply to him, "What

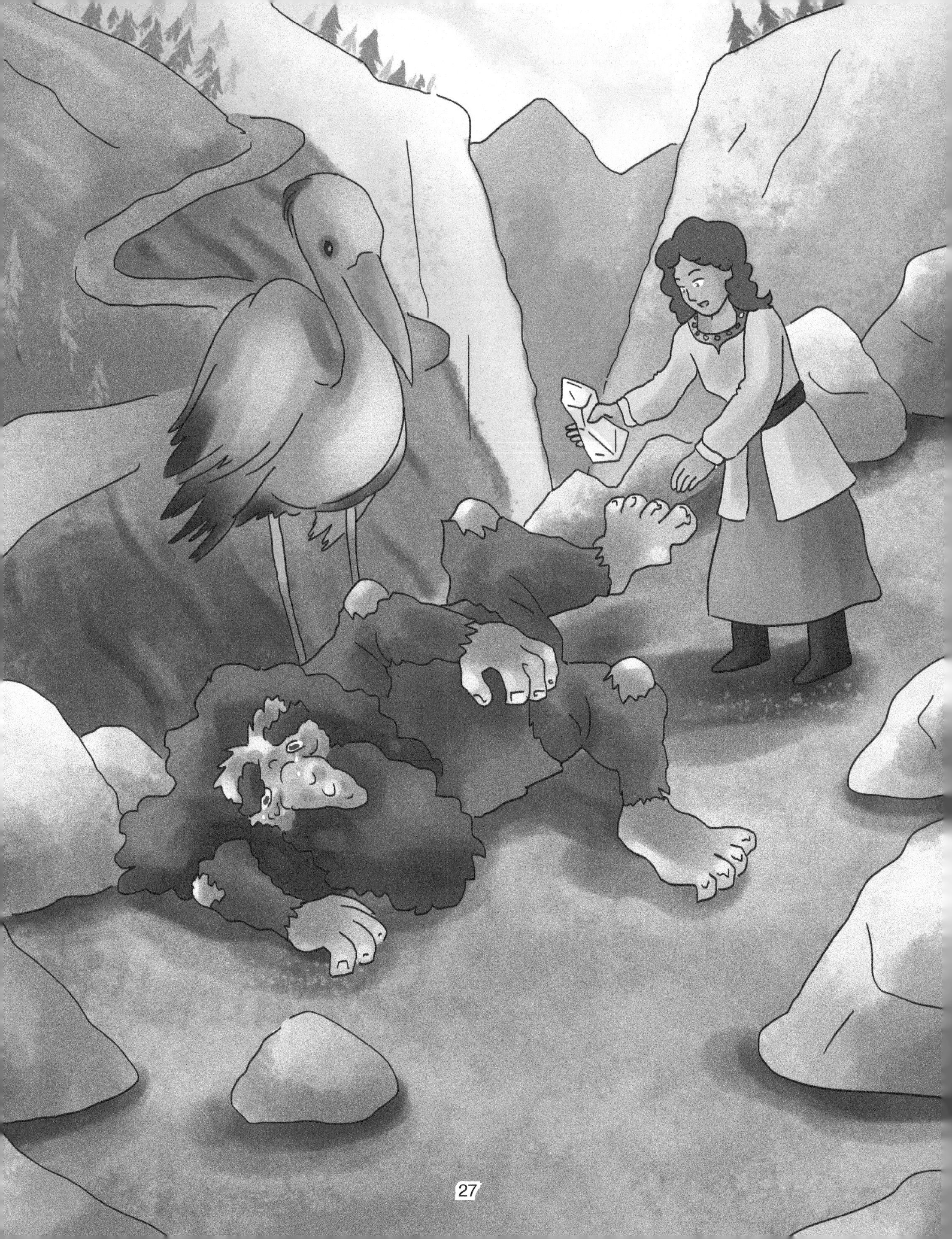

good are all those crystals to you now, you merciless miser? You cannot even move, let alone hike into the valley for one of your crystals."

The troll looked up at her, tears streaming down his craggy old face.

"I am a human and must think like one," declared Kirsten. "So I will have mercy on you and fly into Crystal Valley to bring a healing crystal to you on one condition."

"What is that?" asked the broken old troll.

"That you must allow all of us to share in the gift of healing that God has bestowed on us all," Kirsten demanded.

"If I don't agree, you'll just leave me?" queried Grådig

"That's right!" she stated sternly.

"Then take pity on me and bring me the healing I need to survive," he answered.

Kirsten and the heron soon returned with an extra large, especially powerful crystal. "Such a big crystal for me?" asked Grådig.

"Why, yes, you need a huge amount of healing," she responded. First, she gently rubbed the crystal on his broken bone, his bumps and bruises, his scrapes and slashes; then, she placed it firmly on his chest centered above his heart. "Not done yet!" she stated firmly as she began rubbing it all over his head. "You not only need a change of heart, but, also, a change in your thinking!"

His body began to regain its strength, and his face warmed with a smile. "You have given me the gift of life even though I did not deserve it. Why?"

"God has given all of us the gift of life and of love. These crystals are here to remind of us that He loves all His creation, even gnarly old trolls. As you have been shown mercy, with your healed head and heart, we expect you to keep your word and show mercy to all of us. And as a bonus, the king has provided you with ongoing gifts of rømmegrøt to go with all those mosses, beetles, bugs and slugs you eat up here!"

From that day on, no more was heard the roar,

"Mine! Mine! These crystals are all mine!
I'll keep all their power so I can live a long, long time."

Afterword

Throughout this Norwegian troll tale, Grådig wishes for and eventually receives some rømmegrøt. This is a special creamy porridge that has been made and shared from generation to generation, especially when celebrating weddings and Norway's Midsummer Day festival. Traditional Norwegian weddings lasted three days, and on the third day of the wedding, the new bride was to make the traditional rich sour cream version of this dish for the wedding guests. She and the new husband would eat this porridge using chain-linked wedding spoons to symbolize their unity while the master of the ceremony would make fun of all the problems the bride encountered in preparing the ceremonial pudding dish.

Traditional rømmegrøt is prepared from raw cream that has been allowed to sour. Since raw cream is difficult to find in today's world, this traditional treat has been Americanized in *Time-Honored Norwegian Recipes* published by Penfield Books in 2004. Here is their version of this traditional treat.

Rømmegrøt, Cream Porridge

3 cups of whipping cream

1/2 teaspoon salt

2 cups flour, divided

8 cups of milk, boiling hot

sugar/cinnamon mixture

In a heavy saucepan, heat the cream for ten minutes, stirring frequently so that it will not burn. Sift in 1/2 cup flour, beating to make a thin porridge. Let it boil slowly until the butterfat starts to rise. Reduce heat, and skim all butter off with a spoon. Put it in a cup to keep warm. Now, gradually sift in the rest of the flour, turning up the heat a little and stirring well. Add hot milk gradually, stirring constantly. Next, stir in the salt. It will thicken as it stands. Pile it into a large serving bowl and scoop a hole into the top. Pour some of the butterfat into it, letting it run down the sides. Dish into individual serving bowls and sprinkle on the cinnamon and sugar mixture.

About the Author

The photo credit goes to Greg Cook
of Tumwater, Washington.

Lanette Gutierrez grew up in a small Norwegian community in the Northwest where that cultural heritage was kept alive through arts, crafts, songs, ethnic food and clothing, folktales, holiday traditions, an amazing collection of hand-carved trolls, country life, and, of course, a tradition of faith. After many years as an educator, researcher, and speaker in fields that have included early childhood, family literacy, and teacher education, she is now enjoying writing folktales from the Norwegian traditions of her past to share with her grandchildren, great-grandchildren, and all children who share an interest in Nordic tales from "Once upon a Time."

CPSIA information can be obtained
at www.ICGtesting.com
Printed in the USA
LVHW071751090819
627145LV00010B/34/P